Copyright Matthew C
202
Edited by Lii
All rights reserved. No part of this book may be reproduced in any form or by any means, except by inclusion of brief quotations in a review, without permission in writing from the publisher.

This book is a work of fiction. The characters and situations in this book are imaginary. No resemblance is intended between these characters and any persons, living or dead.

This book is sold subject to the condition that it shall not, by way of trade or otherwise, be lent, resold, hired out or otherwise circulated without the publisher's prior consent in any form or binding or cover other than that in which it is published and without similar condition including this condition being imposed on the subsequent purchaser.

Published in Great Britain in 2023 by Matthew Cash Burdizzo Books Walsall, UK

STROMBOLI

MATTHEW CASH

STROMBOLI

BURDIZZO BOOKS 2023

STROMBOLI

STROMBOLI

For my mum who experienced more than her fair

share of real-life horror

STROMBOLI

STROMBOLI

Some of this is true

STROMBOLI

STROMBOLI

**PART ONE:
DOODLEBUG**

STROMBOLI

STROMBOLI

RAID

He always runs when he hears the sirens —
well, as fast as his one good leg
and his considerable weight will allow.
This time they wail in the middle of tea.
It's nothing special, just toast; there's a war
on, after all.
When he got back home
after the first time
his dad thrashed the living shit out of him.
His mum had been beside herself with
worry;
his dad needed to give her a couple of slaps,
too
only to calm her down, like.
But Malcolm can't stand being trapped
beneath the flowerbed in the air raid shelter.
Beneath the flowers is where Laurie lies.

STROMBOLI

FAREWELL

The whole town made a right song and
dance of it that day, the local regiments
parading up and down the high street
before setting off for France
It was as though the King himself had come
Flags and banners emblazoned with the
regimental regalia fluttered in the wind
A brass band heralded our brave boys as
they marched off to fight for our country
Malcolm's mum, dad, and baby brother
Laurie had a great spot
At the front.
Right at the front
Mum had made a ridiculous number of
ham sandwiches and Dad brought some of
his special brewed ale to share with the
other poor, unfortunate men who hadn't
been allowed to fight
Laurie gawped in wonder and waved his
Union Jack like Billy-o at the soldiers, at the
band
At *everything*.

BAYONET

Malcolm eyed the soldiers' rifles,
in particular, the bayonets.
He liked knives very much.
Liked the way things seemed to magically
part whenever you ran a blade across
something,
the give and then the slippery ease when
you stabbed them into stuff.
He fantasised about the soldiers' bayonets,
wondered how many of them would be
thrusting into German flesh
And how many of the soldiers would enjoy
it.

STROMBOLI

FLAG

He was fed up with Laurie whacking him in the face with his flag
so whilst his brother watched the marching men he found the little piece of skin on the back of his upper arm and pinched it as hard as he could.
Malcolm has pinching down to an art form. Sometimes Laurie doesn't even know what has happened.

STROMBOLI

PINCH

Laurie let out a high-pitched squeal and grabbed his arm.
He ran to their mum, who immediately checked the vicinity for bees and wasps.
Laurie was so little, he could barely string a sentence together so most of what spewed from him was little more than baby talk.
Mum couldn't see any visible marks or bites aside from a pink area where Malcolm had pinched him.
He knew no one had seen him, and,
as Dad always cut their nails on Monday mornings,
no little half-crescent indents should give him away.
Laurie sat on Mum's lap to be comforted
While Malcolm took his place
At the front.

STROMBOLI

PROCESSION

Laurie froze mouth wide open
The procession had barely begun.
The foot-soldiers led the way for a convoy of trucks,
motorcycles with sidecars, and other vehicles.
It was never-ending, a military street carnival,
snaking down the hill and around the corner.
Soldiers waved and blew kisses.
The crowds returned their love,
purveyors stood proudly in their shop doorways,
their finest produce on display.
The sun glistened on polished brasses, buckles and blades.
Laurie's tears stopped abruptly at the approaching thunder.

STROMBOLI

TANKS!

"Tanks!" he yelled,
arms raised,
his face alight with wide-eyed glory,
looking at their parents for confirmation.
"Tanks!"
"That's right, boy," Dad said,
"best ones in the world.
We'll blow them Jerries to kingdom come."
"Gingdum gum!" Laurie cheered, slid off
Mum and landed on his feet, flapping his
arms and his flag.
The Robinsons stood beside them; Mrs
Robinson beamed down at Laurie and
nodded at Mum and Dad.
She gave Malcolm that special smile that
most people around there gave him,
the one that never quite reaches their eyes,
the one laced with either pity or horror.
"He's a bonny young man, Jean,"
Mrs Robinson said, with a ruffle of Laurie's
blond hair.
Malcolm wondered what she'd said about
him when he was that age, or whether that
special smile had even been in use then.
She was the last person to speak.
She, not Malcolm, was the last person to
touch Laurie.

STROMBOLI

GREAT IRON WAR MACHINES

The noise of the tanks drowned out all other
sound.
They couldn't even hear the band.
The people,
especially the children,
went wild
as the great iron war machines trundled up
the hill.
Even Malcolm was impressed by their size
and their capacity for such immense
destruction.

COLOURS

No one saw Laurie break away from the crowd.
They were too busy staring at Mum, who lay stretched
across the road, flat on her face,
her dentures in pieces in the gutter.
But then, when they saw what she was reaching out for,
who she was reaching out for,
they noticed the explosion of colour.
They saw the mess the tank had made.

V1

Malcolm lies in the long grass of Swannies Field and watches the German bombers overhead.
He would rather take his chances out here than down in the confined darkness where Laurie could get him.
They won't bomb an overgrown field.
As that thought crosses his mind he sees something drop from one of the planes and a few seconds later hears a deep, rumbling buzz.

STROMBOLI

BOMB

Malcolm stares in morbid fascination as the bomb,
which resembles a small, futuristic aeroplane,
tears through the sky.
It flies over his field,
just as he suspected it would.
He'd read in the newspaper about what to look for,
what to listen out for,
and how, when the buzzing was over, the V-1 had landed.
The buzzing continues for a few seconds as the rocket vanishes beyond the treeline and then he hears the loud bang.
He hopes the bloody thing lands on the church so they won't have to go on Sunday.

DUD

Unfortunately for Malcolm
the doodlebug misses the church but he is
over the moon when Dad tells him it hit the
school instead.
Malcolm tries not to let his amusement
show.
He dreams of endless days doing nothing
but his father knows better.
"Landed in the playground," Dad says with
a malicious cackle.
"Didn't go off. Was a dud. German
manufacturers for you."
Malcolm fights to contain his anger and
hobbles off to school.

STROMBOLI

MARK

Brian Briggs,
one of the younger kids,
asked about his birthmark on their first day
at school.
"What's that all over your face?"
Malcolm knows,
now he's older,
that Brian wasn't being callous,
just full of genuine childish curiosity,
but that didn't stop Malcolm from making
his life unbearable.

STROMBOLI

COPPERKNOB

He walks along the canal towpath,
where his bad leg makes his foot scuff up clouds of dust,
and where he spots Brian Briggs' tell-tale ginger hair.
He increases his pace.
Brian's whole family are copperknobs, even his parents.
Must have met at a copperknob club or something.
For a big lad,
Malcolm is an expert sneaker and Brian doesn't notice anyone is behind him until he feels his satchel being tugged.
Hard.
Malcolm relishes Brian's expressions of recognition, then fear, as he spins him around and yanks his bag away.
"No, Malcolm, please.
You can have my tuck shop money," Brian begs,
before Malcolm lays a finger on him.
He pushes Brian over,
flings his satchel in the canal, and kneels on top of him,
laughing as the air whooshes from his lungs.
The boy immediately begins to cry.

STROMBOLI

Malcolm slaps his cheek so hard spit that
snot splatters his bare knee.
"Lick it off."
Brian shakes his head and receives another
slap.
Slaps are better than punches:
they leave less evidence.
Brian hesitates again,
his breath hitching in his chest,
so Malcolm gives him another one for good
measure.
Broken,
Brian slides his tongue out and raises his
head so he can touch it against Malcolm's
knee.
Malcolm feels himself grow stiff, like when
he watches girls' P.E.
He slaps Brian again and calls him queer.
Malcolm is getting bored of the slapping,
despite the fun of seeing him suffer
and he searches for something more
demeaning to do.
He sits on his haunches and contemplates
dunking Brian's head in the canal for a few
seconds.
The algae is nice and thick,
almost like a solid surface.
It's just asking to be broken.
However, Malcolm has seen the size of the
rats that dip in and out of the water,

knows that if Brian catches anything and he
gets the blame, he'll be sent away
somewhere bad.
Brian writhes beneath him and Malcolm
sees him stare at the horrid red stain on his
face.
People just can't help it,
especially when they get close up.
Even though Brian might well be fighting
for his life,
he can't resist the urge for a closer
inspection of the lurid explosion that
blooms on the bridge of Malcolm's nose and
spreads across his forehead and into his
blond hair.
Noticing this is enough inspiration for
Malcolm.

STROMBOLI

FLINT

He searches the ground and finds a jagged piece of flint no bigger than a cherry tomato.
He shows it to Brian.
Brian is confused,
obviously wondering what Malcolm is planning on doing,
then he tightens his lips and shakes his head.
Malcolm laughs: the idiot thinks he's going to make him eat it.
As he mentally stores that torture for another occasion,
he holds the stone like a hunk of chalk and begins to rub it vigorously over Brian's forehead.
The sound of the boy's scream electrifies him.

STROMBOLI

SPENCER

"Oi, you ruddy hooligan!"
Malcolm snaps his head around and snorts.
It's Danny Spencer, the scrawny lad who
works at the school library,
and he's with one of the girls from the final
year, Sally Gardner.
Malcolm pushes himself off Brian,
pleased with the grazed, bloody mess he
has made of his forehead,
and faces the couple.
He doesn't care that Spencer is almost three
years older and pally with all the teachers.
Malcolm is still a whole head taller and
twice as wide.
"What do you pair want?"
"Leave him alone, Malcolm Sturgess, or I'll
tell Mr Denby,"
Sally says boldly.
"I don't care what you do, you silly tart."
"Don't you call her that!"
Spencer says, trying his best to sound
menacing.
"I'll tell old Denby I saw you pair *at it* in
Dodnash woods,
shall I?"
The pair exchange a frightened glance;
Spencer takes hold of Sally's hand.
"Tell him what you like, Sturgess. I'm sure
he'll believe every word you say."

Malcolm moves towards them and the girl
shouts for them to run.
They do.
Brian, too..
He makes no attempt to give chase.

STROMBOLI

DICKY

Malcolm doesn't know what is wrong with
his leg other than there is something dicky
with the knee joint and it gets him out of P.
E.
It doesn't matter, though:
he can still move without the aid of a stick;
the doctors say they should be able to fix it
when he stops growing.
He wraps the blood-covered flint in his
hankie and puts it carefully in his pocket.

CANE

Mr Denby sighs when he comes out
of his office and sees Malcolm again,
waiting outside.
"What is it, third time this month, Sturgess?"
"Fourth," Malcolm grunts,
purposefully forgetting to add, 'sir.'
He doesn't care how many times he gets the cane,
it only hurts with the first whack.
He marches into Denby's office without
waiting for an invite,
unfastens his trousers,
bares his arse and bends over the
headmaster's desk.
"For heaven's sake, what is wrong with
you?"
Denby sounds tired,
but
he reaches above his desk for the rattan
cane.

LASHES

"Dunno, sir," Malcolm says, and pushes out a loud fart.
"You're an animal," Denby shouts, opening a window.
"Moo."
"You're getting an extra three lashes for that."
As Denby swipes the cane across his fleshy buttocks Malcolm recalls the time he caught Spencer and the Gardner bird humping in Dodnash Woods at the back of Swannies Field.
He remembers Spencer's scrawny white arse and Gardner's yellow knickers.
It always annoys Denby when Malcolm laughs during the caning,
so he makes sure to cackle like a raving mad man.
"Get your mother to wash your briefs, you filthy pig,"
Denby snaps, red-faced, as Malcolm pulls his trousers up, still grinning.
He ignores the headmaster and limps towards the door without a care in the world until Denby adds,
"I've informed your father."

STROMBOLI

HOME

Malcolm takes off his bottle-bottom glasses
and leaves them on the little shelf in the
porch.
He knows what is coming and doesn't want
his spectacles broken.
The world turns to a blur
it's strangely peaceful.
When he pushes the back door open he sees
a brown shape flit across the kitchen,
smells his father's stink:
his soil, his sweat, his home-brewed ale,
and feels his fist connect with his face.

STROMBOLI

HOBS

He staggers back,
holds the door frame for support but
doesn't fall over,
which surprises him.
His father's punches usually knock him out.
Either his dad is losing it or he is getting
bigger.
"You're nothing but a waste of space,"
Dad screams,
and grabs a handful of his hair and throws
him across the kitchen.
Malcolm puts his hands out to cushion his
collision.
His fists bash against saucepans and he
grabs onto the gas hob rings.
He shrieks and finds he can't let go of the
burning metal.

MELTED

"Serves you bloody right,"
Dad says, pulling him and his melted hands off the cooker and throwing him to the floor.
"Maybe you'll keep your hands to yourself now."
Malcolm hardly feels the kick Dad drives into his ribs,
the pain and the smell of his seared flesh are all-consuming.
"Dress his hands, Jean,"
Dad barks at Mum, and Malcolm knows it's over.

STROMBOLI

DOOR

After Mum has bound his hands like boxing gloves and fed him his dinner, the town's air raid sirens wail their warning and Malcolm instantly gets to his feet.
Dad's heavy hands clamp down onto his shoulders,
"No you bloody well don't, not tonight. You've caused enough bloody grief, boy."
Despite his hands being virtually useless, he struggles against his father as he is dragged across the back garden towards the door in the lawn.
That's what the shelter looks like from above,
As though someone has laid a back door on the grass.
The door back to Hell.

STROMBOLI

HOLE

Mum unlatches the bolts and the padlock
and heaves the door open upwards.
"Don't throw —"
Dad shoves him towards the rectangular
black hole and down he goes.
Malcolm tumbles down the steps and lands
in a heap on a floor carpeted with smelly
old hessian potato sacks.
His parents come inside,
close the door, and complete the suffocating
darkness.
Malcolm hears the bolts and padlock close;
he is sure Dad can see in the dark,
and knows he is locked in for the night.
His parents feel around the small space for
the things they know are there.
Mum lights the oil lantern and Dad slumps
into a corner on a pile of old cushions.
He pulls out a rusty tobacco tin and stuffs
cotton wool into his ear holes.
He finds a bottle of his home brew from
somewhere,
pulls the cork with his teeth,
leans back, and shuts his eyes.
Malcolm sits at the bottom of the steps.
Mum offers a solitary smile.
"Sorry, there's nothing down here for you to
eat or drink,

STROMBOLI

unless you want some of Dad's special brew."
Malcolm shakes his head.
The only thing he wants to do with Dad's special brew is smash him in the face with a bottle of it.
He leans against the earthen wall and lets his stinging hands drop to the floor.
He hopes the pain will keep him awake.

STROMBOLI

MOISTURE

Moisture wakes Malcolm,
something cold dribbling down the nape of
his neck.
His parents' combined snores fills the
underground chamber,
the oil lantern offers the merest of flickers.
The place reeks of rotten spuds and
whatever abomination now fills the metal
slop bucket.
Malcolm lifts a bandaged mitt to his neck
expecting to dislodge a slug or an
inquisitive worm but the already dirty
gauze comes back dark wet.
He recoils and falls across the steps.
In the dim orange glow there's a seeping
wet patch where he has been leaning.
Glistening,
clotted clumps ooze down the walls like
Mum's strawberry jam
and they slop to the hessian sacks.
"No," Malcolm moans as the stuff soaks
through the soil.
"Please, Laurie."

STROMBOLI

JAM

Mum's strawberry jam.
That's what Laurie looked like that day.
His clothes that day:
a sky-blue shirt, and brown shorts
burst at the seams and instantly turned red.
A clean piece of Laurie's blue shirt stuck out
of the gore that day, and fluttered merrily
just like the flag he'd been waving moments
before.
He covered so much of the road and that
day, Malcolm knew he would see his
residue trickling from the tank tracks
for the rest of his life.

SOIL

The mess coming through the soil makes
the wall start to cave in,
a bloody,
muddy
landslide.
Malcolm scrabbles up the steps towards the
door,
away from the seeping, mucky red slush of
his little brother.
He hears Laurie's voice in his head,
Rich, as though he is talking through a
throat full of custard,
thick with a slurry of crushed bone and
viscera.
Malcolm hammers his burnt hands against
the door and yells.
The oil lantern shines brighter, and Mum
screams.
"He's trying to dig his way out, the flamin'
brute."
Dad crawls up the steps towards him in a
half-asleep alcoholic rage but Malcolm
doesn't care what he does just as long as
Laurie is gone.

STROMBOLI

ROT

Just seeing the procession of happy school children crossing Swannies Field makes him want to kill.
Oh, how he would love to see a bomber drop one on them right now.
They sing and laugh with their friends and family.
The youngest amongst them stop to pet the horses that graze.
Grateful for another day's schooling.
The closest give him a wide berth when they see him cut his familiar path across the field.
The fear he instils in them is present even alongside their mothers,
something he is particularly proud of.
Most of their fathers have gone to fight for King and Country.
Malcolm wishes his had, too.
One or two of them spot his huge, round,
wrapped hands, and whispers begin to circle.
Their fear begins to lift and switches to bemused curiosity.
He knows what they are thinking.
He can't get us with his hands like that.
He can sense their collective hatred.
They want his hands to get infected,

STROMBOLI

to turn green with gangrene and rot.
Even if he lost both hands he would still
kick them,
still headbutt them,
still bite them,
still rip out every last one of their throats
with his teeth.

STROMBOLI

STROMBOLI PT1

The playground used to be just another battleground,
a haven for mayhem,
theft, and casual torture.
His domain.
But word has got around that the school bully is now even more incapacitated and when he walks onto the school grounds to hover by his usual spot two other boys are already standing sentinel.
He claimed the crater that the doodlebug left in the concrete,
although it was officially off limits
the second the army had finished clearing the dud away.
"Piss off, Sturgess," one says, and Malcolm is stunned.
"Yeah, scram," says the other, bolstered by his friend's bravado.
"This is *our* spot now."
Rage overwhelms,
he feels the blisters on his palms pop and squirt against the wadded material as he fights to make fists.
Then the two boys laugh at him,
which infuriates him even more.
Malcolm has never felt so angry in his life.
He roars at the lads and begins tearing at the bandages with his teeth.

STROMBOLI

"You're bloody pathetic."
He turns and spits a mouthful of filthy
gauze at whoever it is.
It's Danny Spencer butting in again.
The other children gather behind him.
"I'll fucking kill you and your tart."
"No, you won't."
Danny Spencer takes a step towards
Malcolm and pushes him hard.
One of the crater boys was ready to
ambush,
waiting on his hands and knees behind him.
Malcolm tumbles over the boy and rolls
down into the doodlebug hole.

STROMBOLI PT2

Everything goes dark for a few seconds.
He lands badly on his gammy knee and lets out a jet of hot piss.
"Oh my god, he's wet himself," somebody points out, and laughter blossoms.
Malcolm screams obscenities at them and paws two-handedly at the debris around him in the hope of finding something to throw.
"Look at you," Danny Spencer looks down in amusement:
"even the bloody mess on your face gets redder the more angry you get. You're like a bloody volcano."
Spencer scowls.
"It stops now.
Stop picking on people because your brother died.
Stop going off.
Stop erupting.
There's a war on and even though you're the size of a bloody mountain you're no Stromboli."
"He is," a voice calls from the back, "look at all that lava on his face."
Danny Spencer makes no effort to contain his laughter, nor do the children.
They chant 'Stromboli.'

STROMBOLI

Spencer walks back towards the school and almost collides with Mr Denby, who comes out to see what the commotion is about.
Malcolm sees them exchange words and hears the children hush now the headmaster has appeared.
Everyone hears Denby's raucous laugh, no one has ever heard it before.
He bellows, "Stromboli?"
It sticks like all unwanted monikers do, and each time Malcolm hears it, it makes his blood froth and boil.
"Oh, here comes Stromboli."
"Don't worry, you can outrun that volcano, he's slow."
"Stromboli's going to erupt."
"Look at that lava."

STROMBOLI

BENEATH THE GRASS

People stick together,
the air raids become more frequent and his
parents make him spend more and more
nights beneath the grass.
Laurie torments.

STROMBOLI

TROLL

Everyone calls him Stromboli,
even people who he isn't at school with,
and the more you mock your monsters the
less scary they become.
Malcolm is the troll kicked out from under
his bridge,
the vampire cast into the daylight,
and without their fear, he shrinks.
He takes out his rage on household pets and
wild animals when he can catch them, but
his hate for other children runs deep.
A volcano is exactly how he feels when he
gets angry,
As if everything is going to explode from
the top of his skull.

STROMBOLI

BIRTHMARK

The last time he sees Laurie is in the daytime.
He is the one hiding in the boys' toilets for a change,
waiting for everyone else to go home so he won't have to endure the constant name-calling.
What Danny says about his birthmark getting redder when he gets angry is common talk and as he trashes the lavatories he looks in the mirrors to see if it is true.
The birthmark is a lumpy mass of claret.
The usually purple blemish now writhes and flows with miniscule fragments of bone and skin.
Tiny,
half-mashed eyeballs
the size of peas bubble up to the surface of the swamp that is his forehead,
shattered teeth the size of grape seeds reform themselves to make a crude replica of Laurie's face.
Malcolm smashes the mirror before his brother has chance to speak.

STROMBOLI

LAURIE

On his way across Swannies Field he can
hear Laurie through his birthmark.
*"If you were a good big brother it wouldn't have
happened."*
"It hurts, Malky, it hurts."
Malcolm knows the voice isn't Laurie's,
he could barely string a sentence together,
having been only two when he died.
He knows it's guilt.
That pinch.
He drove his brother into the path of the
tank and ever since then he has been
hurting as many people as he can because
of it.
A stabbing pain lances through his head as
though his birthmark really is lava.
Maybe he is wrong, maybe this is Laurie
after all.

STROMBOLI

LAVA

Malcolm falls to the grass and cries out
when he hears Laurie's laughter.
His birthmark throbs and orange leaks over
his face.
He claws at the skin where the lava burns.
It is lava.
He really is Stromboli.
Malcolm cries for his little brother to stop,
says that he is sorry,
but the volcano is in full eruption.
He tears at his school tie and shirt collar to
alleviate the intense heat and screams when
he feels intense pressure all through his
cranium.
His last thought before he explodes into the
trees is:
this is how Laurie felt that day.

STROMBOLI

ERUPTION

The one thing no-one really considered,
when they found fifteen-year-old Malcolm
Sturgess hanging from the big tree on
Swannies Field
was how an overweight lad with a gammy
leg managed to climb to such a height to
hang himself
with his school tie.
People were shocked by Malcolm's
apparent suicide,
not saddened,
not even his parents.
They all knew it was only a matter of time
before Stromboli erupted again.

STROMBOLI

**PART TWO:
STROMBOLI**

STROMBOLI

STROMBOLI

FAT BOY

The night before the first kid is found
Jimmy Morris doesn't dream about the fat
boy with the birthmark on his face
but every night afterwards he does
.

LATE

Jimmy Morris gets up like he normally does
on a Monday morning:
Late.
He blunders through his bedroom
bumping into everything in the seemingly
impossible task of locating the neatly folded
school uniform his mother has put on his
bed the night before
as she does every school night.
Grimy-eyed,
toast crumbs on his tie and blazer,
Jimmy leaves the house and narrowly
avoids the early morning commuters as
they race along the busy road.
Someone got hit by a car along here.
He remembers his mother's warning but
doesn't think it will happen to him.
Luckily for Jimmy he guesses right:
the most he endures where traffic-related
incidents are concerned are rude hand
gestures
squealing brakes and parping horns from
irate motorists whose last-minute reactions
to sleepy, lumbering schoolchildren are
luckily honed to perfection.
Jimmy doesn't really 'wake up,' as it were,
until he tries to cross the green expanse
known as Swannies Field
and finds his way is blocked by

STROMBOLI

blue-and-white
police tape.

STROMBOLI

NATHAN

The boy was one of the year twelves
Jimmy doesn't know him
didn't know him.
He was Year Nine
but he recognises his face when the
pictures start doing the rounds on
Facebook.
Nathan Matthews
a quiet, inoffensive kid
kept his nose clean
had a close-knit circle of friends,
most of whom came from further afield to
go to school.
Nathan was found
purple-faced and strangled
by other stragglers from the locality who
took shortcuts across the public playing
field.
Dragged through long, damp grass by his
school tie,
Theirs was the last school in the county to
still use the old-fashioned ones instead of
the clip-ons like the police use,
until he stopped breathing.
There were no witnesses
no clues
no theories.
Although he was far from popular,

STROMBOLI

Nathan wasn't picked on.

STROMBOLI

IN MEMORIAM

The field is open again by the time school
finishes in the afternoon and out of instinct
more than morbidity Jimmy crosses
Swannies without giving it a second
thought until he passes a sign asking for
witnesses.
He glances back over the field and sees that
a small collection of flowers have already
been left in memoriam.
He feels bad for not thinking of the lad as he
walks over the grass and promises to pay
his respects the following day.
After school, Jimmy always spends an hour
with his great-grandfather.

STROMBOLI

DANIEL SPENCER

At ninety-nine,
widower Daniel Spencer is eighty-five years
older than his great grandson,

lives on his own in a two bed house and
reluctantly accepts home-help twice a day.
Though his body is failing him,
his mind is as sharp as ever, the
cantankerous old bastard.
Jimmy is the only one who doesn't feel his
wrath, mostly because he is happy to sit
there and listen to his great-grandfather's
stories.
Unlike almost all of the other adults in
Jimmy's life,
he doesn't care about the language his
great-grandfather uses.
*"I fought in the Second World War, I'll talk how
I bloody well want."*

Jimmy brings two mugs of coffee and a
packet of biscuits into a room that hasn't
been decorated for nearly half a century.

STROMBOLI

RELIC

A shrunken relic in the huge, high-backed armchair,
Daniel's bottle-bottom glasses make him bug-eyed,
his flat cap gives him an old-fashioned-schoolboy air.
Bony knuckles tighten around the curve of his walking stick and he taps it hard on the floor.
"Mind you,"
he begins, as though plucking at an already picked thread,
"you shouldn't call someone a cunt."
Jimmy sniggers.
"Grandad!"
Even though Daniel is his great-grandfather, he is the only grandparent Jimmy has ever known.
"Hey, don't you go telling me off too.
Get enough off your mum about swearing."
His bright blue eyes shoot at his great-grandson before he carries on with his story.
"Well, when I was a bit older than you, we were based in Africa, thought I was the bee's bollocks, I did.
"I was bigger than anyone else, see? Not this daft little fucking prune,
no sir."

STROMBOLI

Daniel thrusts his stick towards a black-
and-white photo on the wall.
Jimmy doesn't need to look to see his great-
grandparents' wedding photo,
his great-grandfather in his army uniform
was a towering beast of a man.
It really is hard to believe they were the
same person.
"There was a new recruit,
Kennedy, his name was.
Might have been Kinnock.
Was a Jock, anyhow.
Great big fucking cunt, he was."
Daniel hunches over his walking stick and
slides the bottom plate of ancient false teeth
onto his lip.
Jimmy hates it when he does that,
it reminds him of the xenomorphs in the
Alien films.
"Anyway,"
Daniel continues with a suck and a clank,
"me, thinking I was Bertie Big Bollocks—"
Jimmy spits coffee on the carpet.
"Not in the house, son!"
"Sorry, Grandad."
"Where was I?"
Jimmy can't repeat Daniel's words without
cracking up.
"You were on about the big Scottish guy."
"Yes, I was. Great big Scottish cunt he was."

STROMBOLI

Jimmy loves his great grandfather's tales
but sometimes they take an age to tell.
"You shouldn't go calling people a cunt, you know."
"Grandad, I wouldn't."
"I know what you young 'uns are like.
I've heard you!"
"Okay."
"I called this Jock bloke a cunt."
Jimmy bites the insides of his cheeks.
"I went up to him,
poked him in the chest,
and do you know what I said?"
Jimmy shakes his head.
"Do you know what I said?
I said,
'Oi! You know you?
You're a great big, ugly, Scottish cunt, you are!'"
Jimmy is unable to control the laughter and
it escapes in short,
loud bursts.
"Do you know what he did?"
"No, Grandad."
"He fucking knocked me out!"
Daniel hooks a bony fist up in an uppercut,
animated by his retelling of the tale.
"And that's why you shouldn't go calling
people a cunt.
Do you understand?"
"Okay, Grandad."

STROMBOLI

Daniel Spencer's face falls.
"Daft fat bastard threw himself on a Jerry grenade when they flung it at us.
Was blown to pieces, he was.
Saved about six of us.
He was my best friend.
Stupid *Jock* cunt."
Jimmy sees his great-grandfather's eyes turn watery.
Daniel seems to notice, clears his throat, and points to the biscuits.
"Stop hogging the biscuits then, you fat cunt."
Jimmy passes his great-grandfather the biscuits.

STROMBOLI

DREAM

Jimmy's dreams that night are an abstract jumble of senseless images and sounds.
A pathetic volcano eruption
oozes
rather than spews
lava as red as blood down its sides.
Nathan Matthews being dragged through dewy grass by his tie,
his face purple,
his eyes bulging,
whilst Jimmy's great-grandfather repeatedly grumbles,
'Do you know what I said? Do you know what I said?'
a mindless, senile mantra.
And above it all is the laughing face of a chubby blond boy with a bright pink birthmark.

STROMBOLI

JODIE

"Yeah, man, it's totally sad,
I couldn't believe it when Maya told me."
Jodie Chappell's phone is poised by her
mouth as though she is about to take a bite
from it.
Her best friend, Taylor Latham, crackles
from the loudspeaker.
"It's always good to have an admirer."
"Tay, not when he looks like his mum
fucked a rat,
it ain't."
Jodie always speaks to one of her bitches on
the way to school
so she is never truly alone.
So she doesn't think twice
about crossing Swannies Field the day after
a boy from her school was murdered.
It was obviously a one-off attack:
the twatty kid was probably in trouble with
the wrong sort of people,
pissed someone off.
A lot of the year elevens were involved in
drugs.
Some of her mates dated boys in that year
and she knows all about it.
She doesn't know Nathan Matthews but
people don't just murder fifteen-year-old
schoolboys.
schoolgirls maybe,

STROMBOLI

there were a lot of perverts out there.
"They've got flowers and shit where that kid got killed,"
Jodie says as she passes a small floral tribute leaning up against a big tree.
"Did you know him?"
"Nah, mate, but Suzi Phillips' sister's mate Steven reckons he was gay,"
Taylor blurts down the phone, as though it means something.
Jodie seems to contemplate this news.
"He didn't look gay."
Taylor laughs.
"They don't all skip down the road wearing makeup like Lil Nas X, babe."
"Ha-ha, you know what I me— eh, what the fuck?"
She looks down at her school tie, which now hangs over her jumper and blazer.
"What's up? Are you okay?"
Taylor says with sudden fear.
She has begged Jodie not to cut across the playing field on her own.
Jodie laughs and tucks her tie back in.
"It's alright,
I just got dressed like a fucking tramp this morning,
that's all.
Meet me by the Tesco Express?
Think I need an espresso,
I feel like I'm fucking dead."

STROMBOLI

"Yeah, course, babes,"
Taylor says—
and hears her friend welp again.
Jodie's tie is pulled from below her jumper
by an invisible force.
She drops her phone as she is yanked
backwards off her feet.

STROMBOLI

SUSPENDED

She doesn't hit the ground
but
she feels the bones in her neck crunch.
Her fingers claw at her tie, which has
bunched up beneath her jaw.
The pressure against the back of her neck
and head is phenomenal;
only her heels touch the grass.
Her panic intensifies as she cranes her neck
to see her attacker.
There is no one there.
She tries to scream but only strangled
gurgles came out.
Taylor shouts from the phone on the grass
with a baffled concern that quickly turns to
terror.
The nails of Jodie's fore- and index-fingers
dig into the skin of her neck as she tries to
get beneath the fabric of her tie.
Semi-suspended by an invisible force makes
the experience surreal and almost
dreamlike;
even the wounds where her nails have
gouged feel distant.
But when her unseen strangler pulls on her
school tie and drags her
flailing
silently screaming,
through dew and dog shit

STROMBOLI

it all becomes very, very real.

JUST LIKE NATHAN

The next morning they find Jodie Chapell
on Swannies within sight of Nathan
Matthews' memorial flowers
her legs poking out of the long grass at the
dense crop of trees at one corner of the field
her black tights laddered
one shoe six feet away
next to her mobile phone.
Just like Nathan Matthews
She'd been attacked on her way to school
dragged backward by her tie
until she choked to death.
Unlike with Nathan Matthews
there was a witness.

STROMBOLI

POPULAR

Jodie had been a popular girl.
despite making the trip across the playing field alone.
Jimmy knew her,
she was in the same year.
He dreamed of walking her to school.
When he found out she was murdered he felt as if someone had ripped his insides out.
She was beautiful,
the object of his desires since his first day at secondary school.
There was no reason for this to have happened.
Jodie's best friend,
Taylor Latham,
had been on the phone with her when it happened,
they were rarely without their mobiles.
She heard the murder.

STROMBOLI

WASHOUT

School that day is a washout.
Nobody can concentrate on anything.
Jodie is the name on everyone's tongue.
Taylor is absent due to shock and repeated
questioning by the police.

STROMBOLI

NEXT

Swannies Field is cordoned off after Jodie's murder.
Jimmy takes the long way home and picks up a copy of the local evening newspaper on the way to see his great-grandfather.
Jodie looks so pretty on the front page, long blonde hair and eyes that were so scary silver that you couldn't help but stare at her..
He feels tears swell his eyes so he folds the newspaper,
tucks it beneath an arm
and watches as a police car circles the large field.
The field's off limits now and no one is allowed to walk to school alone or by secluded routes.
The buses that pass Jimmy as he slips along the streets heave with parents and protesting teenagers.
Everyone is terrified that they will be next.

STROMBOLI

VOLUME

Jimmy lets himself in to Daniel's,
taking the key from the coded box on the
wall by his front door.
"It's me, Grandad, Jimmy."
"As long as it ain't one of them fucking
nurses,"
Daniel calls from the living room.
The television is playing softly,
sometimes he leaves it on for company,
and this is one of those occasions:
if he were watching it, the volume would
fill the house.

PAPER

"Got you a paper,"
Jimmy says and tosses the Evening Star
onto Daniel's lap,
sports page up.
"Best get my glasses then, lad,"
he says,
shaking out the paper and squinting at a
football player in a blue-and-white kit.
"They're around your neck."
Jimmy hears his voice falter as images of
Jodie Chappell's swollen purple face flash
behind his stinging eyes.
Daniel pats his chest and finds his
spectacles, dangling from a golden chain.
Jimmy rushes into the kitchen.

BOYS DON'T CRY

Jimmy wipes tears away whilst the kettle is boiling.
Daniel is old-school,
doesn't believe boys should cry
despite coming close to tears himself when reminiscing about his war days.
Jodie.
Why Jodie?
Anger flares inside and he imagines what he would do to the murderer if he caught him.
In his mind, it's a man.
Obviously, it's a man.
They always are.
Kid killers.
Overweight or undernourished,
ugly,
bad hygiene,
his only interest is the black urges that control his every waking moment.

STROMBOLI

RAGE

Jimmy thinks of the killer as he pours out two coffees,
thinks about emptying the kettle over his face before stomping on his forehead until it caves in.
"Fuck's sake, not again!"
Daniel's bellow of rage brings Jimmy out of his thoughts of retribution.
He takes the coffees through expecting to see
that his great-grandfather has had an accident or something:
it wouldn't be the first time.
He's angrily stabbing a finger at the newspaper,
which has shed sheets onto the carpet.
"It's okay, Grandad, I'll get them,"
Jimmy says, putting the coffee down and crouching.
"It's not the fucking paper, boy,
it's the kids!"
Jimmy freezes,
hates himself for buying the paper,
hates himself for visiting his great-grandfather.
Then Daniel says something that makes Jimmy fall off his haunches and onto his arse.
"Fucking happening again, ain't it?"

STROMBOLI

BATTLEGROUND

A long silence, then:
"What is?
What's happening again?"

"That fucking field.
"it's a battleground."
"Why? What do you mean?"
"People been killed on there before, long
time ago, before the war."
"What happened, Grandad?"
"Couple of dogs at first,
then a couple of boys...found with their
necks broke."

CURSED

"It was just before I joined up.
I hoped the fucking place would get
bombed.
It's not safe,

too many evil bastards about."
"Jesus,"
Jimmy mutters.
"He won't fucking help you.
Didn't help them boys."
Daniel shakes a finger at Nathan and Jodie's
photos.

"Didn't help them poor fuckers either, did he?"
Jimmy shakes his head.
"Cursed, that land is, fucking cursed.
Was a big battle there hundreds of years ago,
land's been bad ever since.
Probably why the council ain't built a housing estate on it by now.
I bloody hoped the Jerries would bomb the place.
Rotten to the core.
And now look."
Jimmy doesn't believe the field is cursed, the school that perches on its furthermost point excels in every way with its zero tolerance to crime and bullying.
Surely some of that rot would erode the school if such a thing were true?
"They can't be connected."
"Course they are!
Same piece of land, boy!"
"No, I mean the actual murders.
It's not the same person, obviously, it's 2021.
It's coincidence, is all."
Daniel nods.
"Yeah, you're right.
Just stay off it.
Promise me?"

STROMBOLI

THE GIRL SHE'LL NEVER BE

That night, Jimmy finds it hard to go to sleep.
His heart pines for Jodie Chappell,
the girl she was and the woman she will never be;
whether he ever had a hope of playing a starring part in her life is irrelevant now, as it is over.
Over.
When he goes to sleep he's surprised to see the volcano again,
a giant black-brown pyramid looming against a bright blue sky.
It appears dormant,
just like any other mountain,
apart from a small tuft of wispy grey smoke curling from its summit.
He looks down:
his toes are bare
in soil
no, it's not soil, it's sand,
black volcanic sand
and the beach is littered with strips of snake-like fabric.

Jimmy picks one up,
then another
and another,
they're all the same,

STROMBOLI

ties looped into nooses.
The blue sea rushes back and forth and with
it his great-grandfather sighs,
'That fucking field.
It's a battleground.'
This must all mean something,
it has to.
Jimmy rarely dreams,
or at least not this vividly.
The mountain rumbles gently,
as though it's waking up from a short nap.
Behind him, laughter.
A boy's.

STROMBOLI

BOY

He's big and blond and wearing a version of
his school uniform he's never seen before.
It looks old.
There's something wrong with his face,
aside from the ridiculous milk bottle
glasses.
At first glance it looks like a head injury, but
it isn't.
It's enough to make him stare, though, and
when he does, the volcano rumbles louder.
A birthmark that resembles a gunshot,
right in the centre of his forehead,
and spilling over his nose and cheeks.
When the mountain spits fire the boy
laughs
and the blood vessels of his port wine
birthmark seethe and writhe in rhythm with
the flowing lava.

STROMBOLI

HOLLY WILLIAMS

"Look,
this is gonna be the way of things for the
foreseeable so you might as well just stop
bloody well moaning, the pair of you."
Holly Williams stares at her boys' reflection
in the rearview mirror,
daring them to argue.
"But Mum," Iggy says.
It's always Iggy that starts,
his temper is as fiery as his red hair, as fiery
as his mother's.
"We're like fifteen,"
Evan, his twin, butts in.
He never starts an argument but is always
happy to join in.
"*And* we're bigger than you," Iggy pipes up.
Holly sees the twins share a smirk.
"I don't give a shit how big you are,
I'm still your mother, and you'll do as
you're bloody well told.
You may think you're all tough now but
you don't know who the hell it is out there
killing your school mates."
She watches as their smiles fade and eyes
fall.
She knows she has won the argument.
Guilt bubbles up inside her as she checks on
Chrissie sitting in the child seat between
them,

blonde curls drooping over her snoring
face.
"Look,
I know it'll knock your street cred being
brought to school by your mum,
but what choice do I have?"
"Mum, can you drop us off by the—"
"Mum, stop the car," Evan interrupts, and
slaps his mother's headrest.
"Something's wrong with Chrissie!"
Holly tries to concentrate on both the road
and her two-year-old daughter's reflection.
"What? She's asleep."
But as soon as she says it, she realises what
she took for snoring is actually laboured
breathing.
She looks for somewhere to pull over,
she's almost at the twins' school,
by that bloody field,
but at least there's a layby coming up.
"One of you,
try and see if something's blocking her
airway,"
Holly shouts,
speeding up when she notices the blue
tinges around her daughter's lips.
Iggy unfastens his seatbelt and bats
Chrissie's curls from her face.
"Shit, it's her reins, Mum, they're all
wrapped up around her neck!"
"But I haven't even put…"

STROMBOLI

Holly looks to the passenger seat piled high
with Chrissie's nursery things and sees that
her walking harness isn't there.
"Get it off her."
She hears Iggy panting,
hears the click of Evan's belt coming
undone,
and checks the road behind her is clear
before carefully braking and hitting the
hazard lights.
The whistling sound of sliding leather fills
the car as Holly unbuckles herself and goes
to climb through to the backseat.
For a second she wonders why her boys
have stopped trying to free their sister but
then she sees them fighting with their
seatbelts.
They're wrapped around their throats like
nooses,
the metal buckles jabbing deep into each
boy's oesophagus.
Chrissie's eyes are open now but they're red
with burst blood vessels.
Her little fingers claw at her ears.
Holly throws herself between the driver
and passenger seats and feels hands around
her mouth and neck.
She is pulled back with such a force that
her head cracks the windscreen.
The car starts moving again as an unseen
weight forces itself down on top of her.

STROMBOLI

She's upside down,
head by the pedals,
cold, dead, invisible fingers crushing her windpipe.
Her feet kick at the roof,
the rearview mirror snaps off,
and the car bumps and rocks
as spectral hands take her life.

CLOSURE

The Williams' deaths close the school for the day.
Morbid onlookers,
ninety percent of whom are pupils that should be at school,
pass by to look at the damage the car caused as it ploughed through the eight-foot fence around the outdoor swimming pool.
Witnesses,
half a thousand schoolkids,
watched with dumbstruck horror as Holly Williams' black Ford sped across the playing field.
Initially the school told everyone it was an accident but it was soon announced that all four occupants had already stopped breathing by the time the car hit the water.

STROMBOLI

BURNING

Jimmy takes the time off from school to skirt Swannies.
All the entrances are still cordoned off but even from the road he can see that the pile of flowers where Nathan and Jodie were killed has grown considerably.
There's a few others from the school hanging about the shops when he wanders that way to grab a mid-morning snack and that's where he hears about the plans to storm Swannies.
Harj Kaur is there with his younger brother, and they tell Jimmy:
Saturday night.
An unofficial word of mouth thing:
everyone from the school will meet on the field at seven and burn their school ties in honour of Nathan and Jodie.
Jimmy knows that it's a pointless gesture, it won't bring them back,
but understands it well enough.
It will show the murderer they are united and if none of them have ties then the school authorities won't have a lot of choice other than to accept it as a mass uniform change.
"I'll be there,"
Jimmy confirms, bumps fists with the Kaur brothers, and walks off.

STROMBOLI

It isn't until he leaves the boys and
automatically heads in the direction of his
great-grandfather's house that he
remembers his dream and the hundreds of
school ties on the black sand
all tied into nooses.
He hopes to God it's not a sign of things to
come.

STROMBOLI

FLYER

Jimmy knows it's for the best not to tell his great-grandfather about the Saturday night events but he doesn't bank on the hand-drawn flyers kids have been putting through everyone's letterboxes.
"What the fuck is this?"
Daniel shouts when Jimmy shows his face.
The picture is of a striped school tie,
burning in a clenched fist,
A simple design that anyone could replicate even with the most basic artistic skills,
which is probably the point.
Bold black lettering announces:
MASS TIE BURN
Swannies Field
7pm
For the Victims
Jimmy takes the leaflet from Daniel's trembling fingers. He feels protective towards his fellow pupils and is proud of the stand they're prepared to make against the mysterious maniac who has killed two of their friends,
and against the school authorities,
who still haven't banned the school tie despite their being used in the two murders.
"We're making a stand, Grandad,"
Jimmy says,
crumpling the flyer.

"Against who?"
"The nutter that killed Nathan and Jodie."
Daniel shakes his head in disbelief.
"It's crazy,
stupid.
What if it happens again?
What if someone else gets killed when all this is going on?"
Jimmy laughs and stops when he sees his great granddad's anger.
"Look, there's going to be several hundred of us, probably.
If anything happens, do you think they'll get away with it?"
"I've told you not to go back on that field. It's wrong, that place."
"And with all due respect, Grandad, I don't have to do what you tell me."
Daniel averts his eyes,
clearly hurt by Jimmy's words.
"Oh, it's like that, is it?
I'm just some loony old man?
Do your fucking homework, son,
you'll see others have been murdered on that fucking field."
"Grandad, look, I'm sorry, I believe you, but—"
"Freddie Laurence, the third of August, 1940—"
"Grandad—"

STROMBOLI

"Davey Grinton, the fourth of August,
1940—"
Daniel taps his walking stick on the floor in
time with each syllable.
"Sally Gardener," Daniel shouts, crying,
"my girlfriend, the love of my life,
fifth of fucking August, 1940.
I signed up a week later."
Jimmy is shocked but still knows that it's all
coincidence,
it has to be.
"Grandad, I'm sorry,"
he begins, but Daniel is past listening.
"That was after all our dogs escaped and
were found slaughtered on the grass."
"What do you mean, 'all our dogs'?"
Daniel can't make eye contact,
he stares at a sideboard like it's a window
into the past.
"Every fucker who went to that school who
had a dog.
We kept them outside in those days,
that was the done thing.
They all escaped,
something called them and lured them to
Swannies.
One of the travellers that used to let their
horses on the grass found them,
so they got the blame for a while.
End of September, it was.
Fifteen dogs with their necks snapped."

Jimmy is speechless.
He wants to believe his great-grandfather
but everything sounds ridiculous,
too far-fetched.
"Now it's happening again."
"Grandad, it's 2021,
we've gone through bloody covid,
there's no way this can be connected.
The killer would have to be the same age as you,
for fuck's sake!"
Jimmy hardly ever swears in front of Daniel,
despite the old man's own bad language,
and he instantly feels bad.
A grey watercolour wash of confusion
taints Daniel's face and it scares Jimmy.
He looks as though he'll keel over any second.
A stroke,
a heart attack.
"Sometimes,
I forget what year it is."
"It's okay, Grandad."
"It's not okay!"
Daniel swipes his stick, knocking coffee cups to the carpet.
"That place is wrong, cursed, a field of nightmares."
"Yeah, I know all about them,"
Jimmy mutters

STROMBOLI

so quietly he doesn't think Daniel can hear
But he does.
"Affecting your sleep, is it?
Your mates being murdered?"
Daniel says, and it's the first kosher thing
he's said in what seems like days.
"Yeah, in a way.
I mean, I really liked Jodie, the girl who got"
—he swallows the lump in his throat—
"killed, but the dreams are more just weird,
random stuff that don't make sense.
Sure, I see the kids that got murdered, but I
didn't really know them,
but I hear snippets of conversation me and
you have had during the day and there's
just daft stuff that's nonsense like volcanoes
and some freckly fat kid in glasses with a
birthmark smack bang in the centre of his
forehead."
In the chair opposite him, Daniel crumples.
A de-stringed marionette.

MALCOLM

"Grandad!"
Jimmy rushes to his aid.
Daniel's folded up on himself, chin resting on his stomach,
false teeth in his lap.
As Jimmy reaches for the telephone Daniel sits up
slowly.
He points to the twin sets of saliva-soaked teeth on his crotch.
Jimmy notices his great-grandfather has pissed himself during his...*whatever it was*...and doesn't want to touch his teeth but helps him regardless.
"I need to clean—"
"Lishen firsht," Daniel says, pushing his teeth in.
He's greyer than ever,
Jimmy thinks he should see a doctor.
"That explains everything."
"What does?"
Jimmy notices the confusion on his great-grandfather's face again.
"Stromboli," Daniel says.
Jimmy is familiar with the word:
it's pizza topping,
named after a place in Italy or something like that.

STROMBOLI

This further confirms his theory about his
great-grandfather's confusion.
He's lost it.
Sadness fills Jimmy as he mentally prepares
himself to lose one of his best friends.
"Okay, Grandad."
"Don't you fucking patronise me, you
ragged little cunt."
Daniel's outburst takes him by surprise.
"Stromboli weren't his real name.
His real name was Malcolm Sturgess,
and he was the worst kid in the school.
"When God curses you that bad like He did
Malcolm Sturgess, you have one of two
choices in life:
be bullied forever or be the nastiest cunt
you can imagine."
Now it is Jimmy who is confused.
"Who's Malcolm Sturgess?"
"The boy in your dreams.
He was the fattest kid in school,
had a dodgy leg,
and had a birthmark that made him look
like he'd been shot in the face."
"Holy shit."
Daniel nods.
"He was evil,
manipulative,
a bully,
a fucking cunt.

STROMBOLI

Like I say, when the odds are against you
like that
you either beat or be beaten.
He ruled that school."
Jimmy is in shock but still hears words
come from his mouth.
"What happened?"
Daniel smirks weakly.
"Me.
I stood up to him,
came up with a nickname, *Stromboli*,
after the volcano that's always erupting,
due to that lava splat on his ugly mug."
"Then what?"
"Everyone started calling him it,
even the teachers,
it became his name.
It ruined him having the whole school
against him like that. He was defeated
and—"
Daniel went quiet.
"And what? And what, Grandad?"
"Fucking hung himself with his school tie
on Swannies Field."

STROMBOLI

FABRICATION

Jimmy's head is a bazaar of insane thoughts and imagery.
A large part of him wants to prove that his great-grandfather has lost his marbles,
that it's all fabrication.
He makes puny attempts at research using Internet search engines,
— they make it appear so simple in the films —
but can't find any information about
previous murders on the playing field.
Old ordnance survey maps show the field has been there long since before the school was built but there's no history of battles or anything else.
The Williams' family's deaths are still being treated as suspicious,
but are, as yet, unexplained
and this adds fuel to Daniel's crazy insinuations.
Jimmy foolishly confides what he's been told to the wrong people and,
what with the latest crazes in horror flicks,
he is taken seriously and the name
'Stromboli' is whispered down corridors and on the school buses.
More and more flyers for the school tie burning are distributed as Saturday night races forward.

ROSARY

At his great-grandfather's insistence Jimmy
brings him along to the mass burning.
Jimmy makes sure he's wrapped up warm
and snug in his wheelchair and he's even
brought his own ancient school tie to join in
the ritual.
"You sure you want to do this, Grandad?"
"I haven't set foot on this field since 1940,"
Daniel says as he's pushed down the road,
tie wrapped around his gloved hand and
wrist as though it were a rosary.
"I think all this is happening because he's
been calling me.
He wants to get his own back."
Jimmy still thinks it's nuts but hopes that
whatever happens, it will end tonight.

STROMBOLI

SPEECH

As predicted there are hundreds of kids on the field,
and surprisingly,
although it really shouldn't be a surprise with the amount of advertising they did,
a police presence.
Jimmy is shocked to see their headmaster standing before the horde of children;
behind him, a metal firepit.
Jimmy's impressed.
The school are behind it,
they've realised that this thing will happen regardless and it's better for them to support than to fight.
Everyone is in their uniform, and in regimental lines, they queue up and drop their school ties into the firepit.
When Jimmy pushes Daniel toward the front of the crowd he sees a lectern and microphone by the big tree where Nathan and Jodie's flowers lie.
Typical of the head to want to give a little speech afterwards.
The last of his fellow pupils throw their ties in the pyre and Jimmy moves forward to burn his and let his great-grandfather do the same,
the headmaster takes to the stage to say whatever it is he has to say.

STROMBOLI

EXODUS

Jimmy drops his tie on the burning pile and watches it wrinkle as the flames eat it.
Daniel's hand shakes as it hovers over the firepit.
"Curse you, Stromboli."
When he lets go of his tie it hisses and sizzles like meat cooking.
Somebody screams.

STROMBOLI

RISING

All eyes are on the headmaster;
no one runs to help.
He's the only one who is still wearing a tie
and he rises from the stage in perverse
religious ecstasy.
Nothing holds his tie,
nothing that anyone can see, anyway,
and yet still he goes up.
"No!"
Daniel shouts,
barely audible above the children's
screaming.
Mr Cameron,
the head,
is up in the branches of the tree,
legs kicking a death jig.
Jimmy pulls his great-grandfather away
from the scene and sees the school children
drop as one,
all clawing at their necks,
all fighting something they cannot see.
"Stromboli!"
Daniel screams and forces himself from the
wheelchair.
"Stop."
He collapses to knees that can barely
support his weight.
"Take me, take me."

Jimmy grabs him beneath the arms and tries to get him back in the chair but stops when the children lift off the grass.
It only slows him momentarily, though, and he lifts his great-grandfather back into the wheelchair and starts pushing him through the forest of ascending schoolchildren, ignoring their strangled cries for help.
He manages to get Daniel to the edge of Swannies when he feels the constriction around his own throat.
He thrusts the wheelchair one last time and is yanked backwards by an invisible bungee cord.
He is rising.

STROMBOLI

VOLCANO

He is
rising up through the tree with its morbid,
dangling decorations.
Even though it's near dark, Jimmy can see
his great-grandfather watching in horror.
The pressure in his neck increases as he is
brought up to the very top of the tree like
some sick version of a Christmas angel.
Above and behind him, filling his vision,
red explodes like blood.
Like lava.
Like a birthmark.

Author Biography

Matthew Cash, or Matty-Bob Cash, as he is known to most, was born and raised in Suffolk, which is the setting for his debut novel, Pinprick. He is compiler and editor of Death by Chocolate, a chocoholic horror anthology, and the 12Days Anthology, head of Burdizzo Books and Burdizzo Bards, and has numerous releases on Kindle and several collections in paperback.

He has always written stories since he first learned to write, and most, although not all, tend to slip into the many-layered murky depths of the Horror genre.

His influences —from childhood to present day—include Roald Dahl, James Herbert, Clive Barker, Stephen King, and Stephen Laws, to name but a few.

More recently, he enjoys the work of Adam Nevill, F.R Tallis, Michael Bray, Gary Fry, William Meikle and Iain Rob Wright (who featured Matty-Bob in his famous A-Z of Horror title, M is For Matty-Bob, plus Matthew wrote his own version of events, which was included as a bonus).

He is a father of two, a husband of one, and a zookeeper of numerous fur babies.

You can find him here:
www.facebook.com/pinprickbymatthewcash
https://www.amazon.co.uk/-/e/B010MQTWKK

STROMBOLI

Other Titles by Matthew Cash

STROMBOLI

PINPRICK

All villages have their secrets, and Brantham is no different.

Twenty-years ago, after foolish risk-taking turned into tragedy, Shane left the rural community under a cloud of suspicion and rumour. Events from that night remain unexplained, memories erased, questions unanswered. Now a notorious politician, he returns to his birthplace when the offer from a property developer is too good to refuse. With big plans to haul Brantham into the 21st century, the developers have already made a devastating impact on the once quaint village. But then the headaches begin, followed by the nightmarish visions.

Soon, Shane wishes he had never returned, as Brantham reveals its ugly secret.

STROMBOLI

VIRGIN AND THE HUNTER

Hi, I'm God. And I have a confession to make.

I live with my two best friends and the girl of my dreams, Persephone.

When opportunity knocks, we are usually down the pub having a few drinks, or we'll hang out in Christchurch Park until it gets dark, then go home to do college stuff. Even though I struggle a bit financially, life is good, carefree.

Well, it was.

Things have started going downhill recently, from the moment I started killing people.

KRACKERJACK

Five people wake up in a warehouse, bound to chairs.

Before each of them, tacked to the wall, are their witness testimonies.

They each played a part in labelling one of Britain's most loved family entertainers a paedophile and sex offender.

Clearly, revenge is the reason they have been brought here, but the man they accused is supposed to be dead.

Opportunity knocks, and Diddy Dave Diamond has one last game show to host — and it's a knockout.

KRACKERJACK2

Ever wondered what would happen if a celebrity faked their own death and decided they had changed their minds?

Two years ago, publicly shunned comedian Diddy Dave Diamond convinced the nation that he was dead, only to return from beyond the grave to seek retribution on those who ruined his career and tainted his legacy.

Innocent or not, only one person survived Diddy Dave Diamond's last ever game show, but the forfeit prize was imprisonment for similar alleged crimes.

Prison is not kind to inmates with those type of convictions, as the sole survivor finds out, but there's a sudden glimmer of hope.

Someone has surfaced in the public eye claiming to be the dead comedian.

FUR

The old-aged pensioners of Boxford are set in their ways, loyal to each other and their daily routines. With families and loved ones either moved on to pastures new or maybe even the next life, these folk can become dependent on one another.

But what happens when the natural ailments of old age begin to take their toll?

What if they were given the opportunity to heal, and overcome the things that make everyday life less tolerable?

What if they were given this ability without their consent?

When a group of local thugs attack the village's wealthy Victor Krauss, they unwittingly create a maelstrom of events that not only could destroy their home but everyone in and around it.

Are the old folk the cause or the cure of the horrors?

STROMBOLI

YOUR FRIGHTFUL SPIRIT STAYED

Something happened deep in Charlie's past to make him the way he is. Something causes the visitations, the disturbances, the ghosts. Is it something in his current life or something from a previous existence? Something haunts Charlie, has followed him for years. Something relentless and unstoppable. Something that only wants to torment, torture and ruin. Something that will chase him to the grave.

THE GLUT

FREE YOURSELF

What would you do if you found out your compulsions were not your fault?

That something else had been controlling you all along?

What would you do if you discovered there was a dark part of you, a part of humanity, that was put there by an entity older than the stars?

Vince is binge-eating himself into an early grave. He cannot resist the voice inside that encourages him to gorge, an instinctive reaction to every strong emotion. Finding it increasingly more difficult to live with, he vows to do anything to rid himself of it.

Even if it means stooping to new lows and levels of degradation of which he never considered himself capable.

STROMBOLI

THE DAY BEFORE YOU CAME

When Philippa spots the bungalow it's love at first sight — and she is filled with the sense of safety and warmth whenever she's there. She's not a believer in the supernatural, unlike her best friend, Niamh, but she has to admit there is an energy about the bungalow, a vibrancy that fills her with joy.

Her boyfriend, Ryan, is an angry waste of space, a compulsive liar and petty criminal. He's not frightened of anything - living or dead.

THIS IS NOT YOUR HOUSE

Roger and Vera have been married for years. Everything is a slog, everything is a burden, to Roger, anyway. Having to spend the majority of his life living with his elderly mother-in-law is enough to make anyone bitter.

Vera puts up with her husband even though he doesn't hear the strange noises in the house.

The everyday tedium continues until Roger devises a way to get rid of his mother-in-law.

Other Releases by Matthew Cash

Novels
Virgin and the Hunter
Pinprick
FUR
Your Frightful Spirit Stayed
The Day Before You Came
The Glut

Novellas
Ankle Biters
KrackerJack
KrackerJack 2
Clinton Reed's Fat
Illness
Hell and Sebastian
Waiting for Godfrey
Deadbeard
The Cat Came Back
Frosty

Short Stories
Why Can't I Be You?
Slugs and Snails and Puppydog Tails
OldTimers
Hunt the C*nt
Werwolf

Non-fiction
From Whale-Boy to Aqua-man

Anthologies Compiled and Edited by Matthew Cash of Burdizzo Books
Death by Chocolate
12 Days STOCKING FILLERS
12 Days: 2016
12 Days: 2017
The Reverend Burdizzo's Hymnbook*
SPARKS*
Under the Weather [with Em Dehaney & Back Road Books]
Burdizzo Mix Tape Vol.1*
*With Em Dehaney
Corona-Nation Street

Anthologies Featuring Matthew Cash
Rejected for Content 3: Vicious Vengeance
JEApers Creepers
Full Moon Slaughter
Full Moon Slaughter 2
Down the Rabbit Hole: Tales of Insanity
Visions From the Void [edited by Jonathan Butcher & Em Dehaney]

Collections
The Cash Compendium Volume One

The Cash Compendium Continuity
Come and Raise Demons [poetry]
Website: www.Facebook.com/pinprickbymatthewcash

Copyright © Matthew Cash 2023

Printed in Great Britain
by Amazon